My Pretty Pink
Bible
Sticker Purse

Have fun completing the sticker and coloring
activities! Pull out the sticker sheets and keep
them by you when you complete each sticker
activity page. Have fun!

make
believe
ideas

God made the **world!**

God made the land and all
of the beautiful flowers,
trees, and plants.

Color leaves on a tree.

Color and **sticker**
beautiful flowers.

God made the daytime!

Sticker friends having fun in the park.

God made the nighttime!

Color a bear to cuddle in the dark.

God made the animals, from big cats to small, fluffy cats!

Find the missing animal stickers.

Color Pony and sticker her missing apples.

5

Decorate the frame with **heart** and **star** stickers.

Draw your favorite animal in the frame.

God made all the fish that swim in the sea.

Color and decorate the fish.

Use your stickers to complete the fish patterns.

God put Adam and Eve in a garden called Eden.
It was a beautiful place, full of flowers and trees.

Color and sticker
beautiful flowers in the garden.

A snake tempted Adam and Eve to eat the fruit from God's forbidden tree.

Sticker apples on the tree.

Color the snake.

Noah took his family and two of each animal into the ark to keep them safe.

Sticker Noah and the missing sheep.

Color and sticker food for the ark.

sticker Noah's missing animals.

All of the animals went into the ark, both big and small!

Color the elephant.

Find stickers for the
missing animals.

God made it rain and rain.
Soon the Earth was
covered in water!

Sticker raindrops.

Sticker more fish in the sea.

15

Make Mother Bunny nice and warm in the ark.

Decorate her blanket with flower and heart stickers!

Sticker 2 baby bunnies.

the rain stopped and the ark found dry land!

Sticker the missing animals.

God sent a **beautiful** rainbow as a promise that He would not flood the Earth again.

Color God's rainbow in the sky.

Sticker animals playing in the sun.

Joseph had a **special coat** that his father gave him.

His brothers were very jealous. they wanted special coats too!

Make Joseph's coat bright and colorful.

Sticker more playful rabbits.

Do you have some very special things?

Draw and color them here.

Draw something special in this box.

Color and decorate the special dress.

Add a pattern to the shoes.

Joseph was put in prison in Egypt.
He explained the dreams people had.

Seven fat cows meant
seven years when they
could grow lots of food.

Sticker the missing cows.

Seven thin cows meant seven years of famine, when they could grow very little food.

Color the thin cows.

Joseph helped the people of Egypt store *food* for the famine.

One day, an Egyptian princess found Baby Moses by the river.

the princess took Moses and looked after him as if he was her own son.

Find the missing stickers.

Color the water reeds.

God spoke to Moses from a **burning bush**.
Moses led God's people out of slavery in Egypt.

Color the burning bush.

Sticker a staff for Moses.

David was a **shepherd** boy. He was very brave.

He protected his father's sheep from lions, wolves, and other wild animals.

Color a fierce lion.

David's people were fighting the Philistines!

Goliath was a tall, strong Philistine soldier.

David put a stone in his sling, and hurled it at Goliath.

Find the missing stickers.

David's stone hit **Goliath** between the eyes and he fell down dead!

The Philistines ran away.

Use your **stickers** to decorate Goliath's shield and sword.

An angel came to **Mary** and gave her amazing news.

"You will have a very special baby. He will be the son of God."

Color a beautiful angel.

Mary gave birth to Jesus in a stable.

Draw and color
Jesus' bed.

Use your stickers to
finish the animal patterns.

A special star shone over the stable in Bethlehem.

Draw and color this amazing star.

Sticker stars too!

An **angel** appeared to shepherds in a **bright** light.

She told them to go to Bethlehem, where God's special king had been born in a stable.

Sticker more sheep on the hill.

Three wise men followed the bright star to find Jesus.

Myrrh

Sticker a bright star.

Gold

Frankincense

Color the three gifts and decorate them with stickers.

All of the **animals** gathered around the **baby** Jesus.

Color the stable and the animals.

Jesus grew up to be a wise man and he performed miracles!

Color the fish.

Jesus fed thousands of people with only a few fish and loaves of bread. People were amazed. This was a great miracle.

Sticker the missing loaves!

God gives us lots of food to enjoy.

Draw your favorite meal on the plate.

Color the drink.

Draw your favorite treats in the jars.

Sticker more yummy treats.

Jesus died so that we can be God's friends.

Draw your best friend in this picture frame.

Sticker more best friends.

Draw a group of friends in this picture frame.

God loves you.
You are special.

Draw a Picture of yourself.

Draw things you love
to do in here.

use stickers to decorate the Pictures.

God gives us our family to love and care for us.

Draw your family at home.

Sticker balls for the dogs to play with.

Where in the World do you live?

Write your answer on the flag.

Write the town you live in here.

Draw your house here.

Jesus' birthday is on Christmas day.

When is your birthday?

Sticker candles on the birthday cake!

Color the cake and presents, then decorate them with stickers.